ME, MYSELF AND I

Book & Lyrics
by
Alan Ayckbourn

Music
by
Paul Todd

SAMUEL FRENCH, INC.
45 WEST 25TH STREET   NEW YORK 10010
7623 SUNSET BOULEVARD   HOLLYWOOD 90046
LONDON   *TORONTO*

CAST

The play was written for a cast of 3 women and one man.

MARY YATELY

who frequently divides herself into: —

ME

MYSELF

I

* * *

RODNEY BEECH, a reporter

who looks not dissimilar to: —

BILL YATELY, her husband.

* * *

Scene: A bar at lunchtime.

4

SONG BREAKDOWN

TITLE	ME	MYSELF	I	MAN
RECIT 1	X	X	X	X
SOMEBODY NEW	X	X		X
SONG OF MY CHILDHOOD	X	X	X	X
I DON'T WANT TO DO IT	X	X	X	
MY HOUSE	X	X	X	X
UNLIKELY	X	X	X	
WIFE SWAP DANCE	X	X	X	
OPEN FOR LOVE	X	X	X	
ME MYSELF AND I	X	X	X	X
RECIT 2	X	X	X	
NO MORE	X	X	X	X
ELECTRIC WOMAN	X	X	X	
CLOSER			X	X
TEACHING THE CHILDREN		X		
RECIT 3/WHERE	X	X	X	
HAVE YOU EVER THOUGHT?	X			X
ANOTHER BITE	X	X	X	X
ME MYSELF AND I (reprise)	X	X	X	X
	14 + 2	11 + 5	12 + 3	10

ME, MYSELF, AND I

ACT I

[MUSIC #I – 1(a): *RECITATIVE I*]

REPORTER.
INTRODUCING RODNEY BEECH
YOUNG, PROMISING REPORTER
(THREE A LEVELS)
FROM THE EVENING ECHO.
NOTEBOOK POISED AND READY FOR ACTION.
ABOUT TO INTERVIEW: —
  ME.
MRS. M. YATELY,
MOTHER OF FOUR
(NO A LEVELS)
OF FOURTEEN CALDICOTT GARDENS,
NETTLEFORD ESTATE,
EAST HOPLEY,
NEAR NETTLEFORD,
NORTH YORKS.
(WITH A POST CODE I CAN NEVER REMEMBER)
ABOUT TO BE INTERVIEWED BY: —
  REPORTER.
RODNEY BEECH. ABOUT TO INTERVIEW MRS. W.
  YAXBY —
OF SOMEWHERE-OR-OTHER GARDENS
WINNER OF THE IDEAL MUM COMPETITION,
ORGANISED BY THE EVENING ECHO,
IN ASSOCIATION WITH NETTLEFORD NURSERIES
AND E. J. COLBY AND SON BRACKETS
  HARDWARE . . .
  ME.
ABOUT TO BE INTERVIEWED
BY MR. RODNEY BIRCH OF THE EVENING PAPER
(I THINK HIS NAME WAS)
FOR WINNING A COMPETITION
I DIDN'T EVEN GO IN FOR.
IT WAS OUR MARJORIE . . .

7

REPORTER.
THE SORT OF INTERVIEW
THAT COULD MAKE A YOUNG JOURNALIST A STAR
OVERNIGHT. HA. HA.
ME.
WHY ME?
REPORTER.
I'VE WRITTEN IT BEFORE I GET THERE . . .
ME.
WHAT DO I SAY TO HIM?
REPORTER.
MY SECRET IS THAT I'M BLESSED
WITH A WONDERFUL HUSBAND
AND TWO WONDERFUL CHILDREN—
ME.
FOUR . . .
REPORTER.
ADMITTED MRS. WENDY—
ME.
MARY—
REPORTER.
YAXBY . . .
ME.
YATELY . . .
REPORTER.
ATTRACTIVE BLONDE—
ME.
BRUNETTE . . .
REPORTER.
AGED THIRTY-SIX . . .
ME.
FOUR . . .
REPORTER.
. . . TOLD ME WITH A SMILE . . .
ME.
. . . A SMILE . . .

REPORTER. Why do they all sound quite so similar . . . ?
ME. Why does it make me sound so boring . . . ?
REPORTER.
MIND YOU . . .

ME.
MIND YOU, MY FRIENDS HAVE SOMETIMES SAID

(*MYSELF and I, her counterparts, join her.*)

ME/MYSELF/I.
THERE'S MORE TO YOU
THAN MEETS THE EYE, MARY . . .
REPORTER.
MIND YOU . . .
ME.
UNFORTUNATELY, IT IS USUALLY ONLY ME
THAT DOES MEET THE EYE . . .
REPORTER.
MIND YOU . . .
ME.
WHICH IS UNFORTUNATE . . .
MYSELF.
HEAR! HEAR!
REPORTER.
MIND YOU, SHE IS A WOMAN . . .
I.
CAN I HELP IT IF I FEEL IT'S ME THAT LETS ME DOWN?
MYSELF.
HEAR! HEAR!
I.
NOT I . . .
REPORTER.
I PRESUME SHE IS A WOMAN IF SHE'S MOTHER
OF THE YEAR . . .
ME.
THERE ARE TIMES I WISH . . .
I.
. . . WISH THAT I, MYSELF . . .
MYSELF.
MYSELF COULD BE . . .
ME.
. . . COULD BE ANYONE BUT ME. ANYONE . . .
MYSELF.
ANYONE.
I.
ANYONE . . .

[MUSIC #I – 1(b): *SOMEBODY NEW*]

ME.
BEFORE I MEET HIM HERE
FOR THE FIRST TIME
COULD I POSSIBLY
FIND A DIFFERENT IMAGE
TO PRESENT TO HIM
FOR THE FIRST TIME?
SOMEBODY NEW,
SPARKLING THROUGH.
DIFFERENT ME,
HOW DO YOU DO?

SO WHEN I MEET HIM HERE
FOR THE FIRST TIME
HE'LL BE HYPNOTISED
BY THIS LOVELY STRANGER.
AS HE CONTEMPLATES,
FOR THE FIRST TIME,
SOMEBODY NEW
HOVING IN VIEW.
DIFFERENT ME,
HOW DO YOU DO?

AND, AS I MEET HIS GAZE,
SUDDENLY HIS HEART'S ABLAZE,
CAUSING THIS ROMANTIC HAZE.
NOTHING WE NEED SAY . . .
I WILL WATCH THE MOON ECLIPSE
AS HE BENDS TO KISS MY LIPS,
THAT'S ANOTHER THOUSAND SHIPS
I HAVE LAUNCHED TODAY . . .
REPORTER.
JUST BEFORE I MEET HER HERE
FOR THE FIRST TIME,
I'M CONSIDERING
HOW TO BEST IMPRESS HER.
SHE'LL BE MEETING ME
FOR THE FIRST TIME,
SOMEBODY NEW,
HOW DO YOU DO?
ONE NEVER KNOWS

WHAT COULD ENSUE.
FOR WHEN I MEET HER HERE
FOR THE FIRST TIME,
I COULD INTRODUCE
THIS AMAZING CHANGE OF
PERSONALITY.
FOR THE FIRST TIME
SOMEBODY NEW,
—NEVER GUESS WHO—
STUNNING PHYSIQUE,
SEVEN FOOT TWO . . .

THE ONLY WORDS SHE'LL SAY—
   MYSELF.
DARLING, YOU MAY HAVE YOUR WAY,
I AM BUT A BALL OF CLAY,
PUTTY IN YOUR HANDS . . .
   REPORTER.
I'LL GIVE MY LOPSIDED SMILE,
WHISPER, "YOU MUST REST AWHILE."
SHOWING I'M A MAN OF STYLE,
ONE WHO UNDERSTANDS . . .
   ME/REPORTER.
COULD WE BEGIN AGAIN
FOR THE FIRST TIME?
ALL THOSE FAULTS WE HAD
SAFELY DEAD AND BURIED?
NOW WE'RE MEETING HERE,
FOR THE FIRST TIME,
   ME.
SOMEBODY NEW—
   REPORTER.
SOMEONE WHO GREW—
   ME.
DAZZLING ME—
   ME/REPORTER.
HOW DO YOU DO?
   ME.
HE'LL MURMUR SWEET AND LOW . . .
   REPORTER.
SHE WILL SCREAM—
   MYSELF.
I NEED YOU SO . . .

ME.
FROM HIS EYES ALONE I'LL KNOW . . .
REPORTER.
AS I SET HER FREE . . .
MYSELF.
THANK GOD, MEN LIKE YOU EXIST . . .
ME.
WITH A DEEP DESIRE, THEY KISSED . . .
ME/REPORTER.
THINK OF WHAT WE MIGHT HAVE MISSED,
OLD-STYLE YOU AND ME . . .

ON THE VERGE OF MEETING HERE
FOR THE FIRST TIME,
WE ARE STRANGERS STILL
LIKE TWO EMPTY BLACKBOARDS
TO BE WRITTEN ON
FOR THE FIRST TIME.
UP TO US TWO
WHAT WE NOW DO.
WHAT WE BOTH WRITE
EACH WILL CONSTRUE . . .
ME.
DIFFERENT ME . . .
REPORTER.
DIFFERENT YOU . . .
ME/REPORTER.
HOW DO YOU DO,
SOMEBODY NEW.
REPORTER.
HALLO . . .
ME.
HALLO . . .
REPORTER/ME.
HALLO . . .

REPORTER. Mrs. Yaxby? It must me. I'm so sorry . . .
ME. Yately.
REPORTER. Mmm?
ME. It's Mrs. Yately . . .
REPORTER. Yately. Of course it is. Yately. Mrs. W. Yately, Evening Echo Mum of the Year. Voted by over a thousand readers. What's the W for? Wendy? Winifred? Wanda?

ME. Mary.

REPORTER. Mary. I see. W for Mary. They got that bit wrong as well, did they? Jolly good. Would you care for a . . . ? (*he indicates his drink*)

ME. No, thank you. Not for me. Not at lunchtime.

REPORTER. No, perhaps you're right. We don't want Mum of the Year seen falling down in the road, do we? (*he laughs*)

MYSELF. Oh, we've got a right little laughing boy here, haven't we?

REPORTER. Anyway. My name is Rodney Beech. How do you do?

ME. How do you do?

I. I think he's rather sweet.

REPORTER. And I'll be writing this little feature about you for this Saturday's edition.

ME. Yes, I see.

REPORTER. So. If you've no objections, we'll get on with it, shall we? (*Producing a pencil and notebook*) Now then, Mrs. Yately — Mary. May I call you Mary?

MYSELF. No.

I. Yes.

ME. Of course.

REPORTER. Thank you. Well, Mary . . . It's Rodney, by the way . . .

MYSELF/I. (*cod sentimentally*) Aaah!

ME. Actually, I thought it would be Mr. Ash.

REPORTER. Mr. Ash?

ME. Who'd be talking to me.

REPORTER. Ah, well, no. Mr. Ash doesn't normally . . . It's not his usual custom to . . .

I. He's too grand for you, dear.

REPORTER. He doesn't come into the field himself all that frequently. We call it the field.

MYSELF/I. Moo!

ME. Oh, it doesn't matter . . .

REPORTER. So I'm afraid you'll have to put up with Mr. Beech instead of Mr. Ash. I hope you won't feel you're barking up the wrong tree, eh? (*he laughs*)

(*ME looks blank. I and MYSELF laugh rather sarcastically.*)

ME. I beg your pardon?

I. It was a joke, dear. The man made a joke.

ME. Oh.

MYSELF. God, she's so dim . . .

REPORTER. Doesn't matter. Forget it. Just a little joke.

ME. Oh. Yes . . . (*she smiles belatedly*)

MYSELF. Mum of the Year . . . flurp . . . flurp . . .

I. Leave her alone.

REPORTER. I'm sorry. It's one of my weaknesses, I'm afraid. Making jokes. I'm sorry.

ME. That's alright, I like jokes.

MYSELF. You never see them.

REPORTER. I'll try not to do it too much.

MYSELF. She just puts them in her bag, takes them home and looks at them later. Wakes up in the middle of the night — (*opening her handbag*) — ha, ha, ha.

REPORTER. Now, this obviously is going to be about you and your family. But mostly I want it to be about you. I want to hear all there is to know about you. Hold back nothing.

ME. Well, I'm afraid I'm not all that interesting.

REPORTER. Oh, come on, that's what they all say . . .

ME. I'm really very ordinary.

MYSELF. Hear! Hear!

I. Rubbish.

ME. Just one of these boring old housewives, you know . . .

I. Shame!

REPORTER. (*admonishingly*) Ah, now . . .

ME. That's me.

I. Don't listen to her . . .

REPORTER. Anyway . . .

I. . . . she's always selling us short . . .

MYSELF. No, she's not. For once, she's actually telling the truth. That's rare I know but —

ME. (*sharply*) Look, please, shut up.

REPORTER. (*startled*) What?

ME. Oh, nothing. I was talking to myself.

REPORTER. Ah. First signs, you know . . .

ME. Yes. (*she smiles*) Sorry . . .

MYSELF. Flurp . . . flurp . . . flurp . . .

[MUSIC #1–2: *SONG OF MY CHILDHOOD*]

REPORTER. Right. From the beginning . . .

REPORTER.
SO TELL ME ALL ABOUT YOUR CHILDHOOD—
ME.
CHILDHOOD? LET'S SEE . . .
REPORTER.
DO YOU RECALL A HAPPY CHILDHOOD?
ME.
CHILDHOOD? NOT ME.
I WAS THE LAST OF FOUR
WE WERE SO VERY POOR WE
RAGGED, GAWKY,
STARVING, DOORKEY KIDS.
REPORTER.
SO FOOD WAS SCARCE?
ME.
WE'D NEVER EAT . . .
REPORTER.
YOU WENT TO SCHOOL?
ME.
IN JUST BARE FEET . . .
REPORTER. (*to himself*)
I SEE IT THERE,
MY RAGGED BAREFOOT CHILDHOOD . . .
MYSELF. (*replacing ME*)
OF COURSE MY FATHER WASN'T HOME MUCH.
REPORTER.
ORPHANED, LIKE ME.
MYSELF.
HE HAD SOME CUSHY JOB IN WHITEHALL
REPORTER.
WHITEHALL? I SEE . . .
MYSELF.
WE HAD THIS VAST ESTATE
MYSELF, MY BRO, MY MATER
(BABS CAME LATER)
QUITE NEAR CATERHAM—
REPORTER.
A VAST ESTATE?
MYSELF.
WELL, MOST OF KENT . . .
REPORTER.
YOU WEREN'T THAT POOR?

MYSELF.
WE OVERSPENT.
REPORTER. (*to himself*)
A TITLE SWITCH . . .
MY LITTLE RICH GIRL STORY—
ME. (*replacing MYSELF*)
HOW IS IT SO FAR?
REPORTER.
IF YOU'LL EXCUSE ME—
I AM
A FRACTION
CONFUSED.
PLEASE, CARRY ON . . .
I. (*replacing ME*)
I SPENT MY EARLY DAYS IN CAIRO
REPORTER.
CAIRO?
I.
WHAT'S WRONG?
REPORTER.
I THINK I NEED ANOTHER BIRO . . .
I.
THEN IN HONG-KONG.
MA WAS A STRIPTEASE QUEEN.
SHE PLAYED THE CONCERTINA.
THERE'S NOT BEEN A
MORE OBSCENER ACT.
REPORTER.
IS THAT A FACT?
SOME THINGS CONFLICT—
I.
BUT ISN'T LIFE—?
REPORTER.
—AND CONTRADICT.
I.
—ONE PARADOX?
REPORTER. (*to himself*)
MY STRIPPER SQUEEZE BOX MOTHER . . . ?
ME. (*replacing I*)
STILL WITH ME SO FAR?
REPORTER.
WELL. I CONFESS YOU
LOST ME

A LITTLE
BACK THERE.
MAY I RECAP?
YOUR BAREFOOT FATHER WORKED IN
  WHITEHALL . . .
THAT BIT SOUNDS WRONG.
YOUR MOTHER STRIPPED HER WAY ROUND
  KENT OR
WAS IT HONG KONG?
YOUR BROTHER HAD NO SHOES—
I FIND THIS MOST CONFUSING,
QUITE BEMUSING.
AM I LOSING TOUCH?
  ME/MYSELF/I.
THAT'S HOW IT WAS
WE ALL AGREE
  MYSELF/I.
WHAT'S RIGHT FOR US
  ME.
SEEMS FALSE TO ME . . .
  ME/MYSELF/I.
IT'S UNDERSTOOD
IT'S JUST A CHILDHOOD STORY.
THAT'S HOW IT WAS
WE ALL AGREE.
WHAT'S RIGHT FOR HER
SEEMS FALSE TO ME.
IT'S UNDERSTOOD
IT'S JUST A CHILDHOOD STORY.

(*ME and REPORTER, seated as before.*)

REPORTER. (*after a pause*) Yes . . . You might have to go a
shade slower for me, Mary. I have shorthand, of course. But it
does have its limits . . .
  ME. Sorry.
  REPORTER. Yes. (*he studies his notes*) Yes, I might have to
come back to you on that later on. Anyway. Now. Children.
You've got how many? Two, it says here. What are they? Boy and
a girl? Two boys? Two girls? I can't think of any other combina-
tions offhand. (*he laughs*)
  MYSELF. It's another joke. Wake up!
  ME. Oh. (*she laughs*)

I. He's lovely when he smiles.

ME. No. Three girls. One boy.

REPORTER. Three . . . ? Then I take it you have four children and not two as it says here?

ME. Yes. Four. (*REPORTER scribbles in his notebook.*) Well, that was the number when I last counted, anyway. (*she smiles*)

(*REPORTER fails to notice.*)

MYSELF. Oh, God. Now she's making jokes. We're all doomed.

I. I thought that was quite funny.

MYSELF. Yes, he's rolling about, isn't he? Him and Marti Caine there.

[MUSIC #I – 3: *I DON'T WANT TO DO IT*]

REPORTER. So I take it, Mary, you're fond of children?

I. No.

MYSELF. Sometimes.

ME. (*smiling happily*) Oh, yes . . .

ME/MYSELF/I.

I DON'T WANT TO DO IT.

YOU CAN'T MAKE ME DO IT

YOU WON'T MAKE ME DO IT,

'LESS I WANT TO DO IT—

ME.

EVER SINCE MY MOTHER

WENT IN LABOUR,

AIDED BY THE MILKMAN

AND A NEIGHBOUR

PRACTICALLY THE FIRST WORDS

I COULD SAY WERE—

I.

I WILL DO NOTHING I DON'T WANT TO DO.

ME/I.

I DON'T WANT TO EAT IT

YOU CAN'T MAKE ME EAT IT.

YOU WON'T MAKE ME EAT IT

'LESS I WANT TO EAT IT—

MYSELF.

EVER SINCE THOSE AWFUL

SCHOOLTIME LUNCHES,

SAUSAGE A LA TOAD WITH
MASH THAT CRUNCHES.
TAPIOCA SERVED IN
STICKY BUNCHES—
     ME.
I WILL EAT NOTHING I DON'T WANT TO EAT.
     MYSELF.
AS A LITTLE GIRL MY SHRILL INSISTANCE
WORE AWAY MY PARENTS' TIRED RESISTANCE,
     ME.
I WOULD OVERRIDE THEIR ADMONITIONS
THREATEN THEM WITH PUBLIC EXHIBITIONS.
     I.
I'D STAND AND YELL
TILL THEY BOTH GAVE IN.
—MISS CRAFTY—
SHE KNEW DAMN WELL
SHE WOULD ALWAYS WIN
BY SCREAMING—
     ME/MYSELF/I.
I DON'T WANT TO DO IT
YOU CAN'T MAKE ME DO IT
YOU WON'T MAKE ME DO IT
'LESS I WANT TO DO IT.
     I.
LATER AS A SPOTTY
TEEN TEMPTATION
I BECAME A SOURCE OF
MALE FRUSTRATION,
AS I MADE THE PO-FACED
DECLARATION—
     MYSELF.
I WILL DO NOTHING I DON'T WANT TO DO.
     MYSELF/I.
I DON'T WANT TO HAVE IT
YOU CAN'T MAKE ME HAVE IT
YOU WON'T MAKE ME HAVE IT
'LESS I WANT TO HAVE IT.
     ME.
THEN I MET A MAN WHOM
I LOVED DEARLY.
THROUGH HIS EYES I SAW ME
MUCH MORE CLEARLY.

THEN IT WAS A CASE THAT
QUITE SINCERELY—
   I.
I WOULD DO ALL THAT HE'D WANT ME TO DO.
   MYSELF.
HE WOULD GIVE COMMANDS AND I WOULD DO THEM
HE'D CREATE THE HOOPS AND I'D JUMP
THROUGH THEM . . .
   ME.
WE HAD FOUND THE PERFECT WAY OF LIVING—
HE'D DO ALL THE TAKING, I THE GIVING . . .
   I.
LIFE HAS A WAY
LIFE REMEMBERS THOSE
WHO CHEAT IT.
LIFE MAKES THEM PAY,
PAY RIGHT THROUGH THE NOSE
FOR SAYING—
   ME/MYSELF/I.
I DON'T WANT TO DO IT
YOU CAN'T MAKE ME DO IT
YOU WON'T MAKE ME DO IT
'LESS I WANT TO DO IT.
   ME.
NOW TODAY THE CIRCLE'S
BEEN COMPLETED
   MYSELF.
I AM CAREFUL HOW MY
KIDS ARE TREATED—
   I.
MAKING SURE THAT HISTORY'S
NOT REPEATED—
   ME/MYSELF/I.
I MAKE SURE SOMETIMES THEY DO THINGS
THEY DON'T
WANT TO DO.

(*ME and REPORTER, seated as before.*)

REPORTER. Yes. I think I'll just put that you have a sane and practical attitude towards children. Not over-sentimental. In fact, a typical ideal mum.
MYSELF. Flurp . . . flurp . . . flurp . . .

REPORTER. Good. And it says here that you live on the Nettle-ford Estate so that can't be right, can it? Not if it's down here?

ME. Yes, that's right. The Nettleford Estate.

REPORTER. Oh, surprise. And your husband?

ME. Oh yes, he lives there too.

REPORTER. (*patiently*) Yes, I guessed he lived there. I mean, what does he do for a living?

ME. (*flustered.*) Oh, I see. I'm sorry.

MYSELF. There she goes. Brain of Britain. Flurp . . . flurp . . . flurp . . .

ME. (*losing control, tearfully*) Listen, will you just shut up and leave me alone. I'm doing my best here . . .

REPORTER. What was that?

ME. . . . honestly I am . . .

REPORTER. Mrs. Yately?

MYSELF. Flurp . . . flurp . . .

REPORTER. Mary . . . ?

I. (*over this*) Leave her alone, for God's sake. She's doing her best, isn't she?

MYSELF. (*simultaneously*) Flurp . . . flurp . . .

ME. (*over this last*) If you think you can do any better, just you try answering all these questions. See how you like it . . .

REPORTER. (*loudly*) Mrs. Yately! (*A silence, more gently*) Are you alright, Mrs. Yately?

ME. (*weakly*) I'm sorry. I just . . . I lost control of my-self . . . Or rather, me lost control of I . . . myself. You see?

REPORTER. Would you prefer it if we carried on tomorrow? If you'd prefer?

ME. No, I'll be alright. Don't worry.

REPORTER. You're sure?

ME. Yes. Please. Carry on.

REPORTER. (*uncertain*) Yes. Well, I was asking about your husband . . . Excuse me, you're not undergoing any sort of— strain, you know, at the moment, are you?

ME. No. My husband works for Regis. Electronics, you know.

REPORTER. Oh, yes. I know the firm.

ME. We're both very happy. Both of us.

I. Liar.

ME. He's always been very good . . . He's marvellous. Won-derful. I think sometimes it's me. I'm the problem, you see. Me. Not him.

I. (*derisively*) Ha!

[MUSIC #I–4: *MY HOUSE*]

ME.
WHO'S THIS IN OUR HOUSE?
THIS HOUSE IS MY HOUSE.
REPORTER. (*as husband*)
HALLO, DARLING. YOU'RE BACK A LITTLE EARLY
TONIGHT.
ME.
SHE'S HERE IN MY HOUSE . . .
REPORTER.
MRS. LEES WAS WANTING—
MYSELF. (*as MRS. LEES*)
I LOOKED IN BECAUSE I NOTICED THE LIGHT.
ME.
. . . LOOKED INTO MY HOUSE . . .
REPORTER.
MY GOLLY, LOOK, TIME JUST PASSES—
MYSELF.
I HEAR THAT YOU'RE TAKING KEEP-FIT CLASSES
NOW . . .
I.
SHE'S HERE IN YOUR HOUSE . . .
ME.
IT'S MODERN DANCE.
I.
SAT THERE IN YOUR HOUSE . . .
REPORTER.
WE WERE TALKING BEFORE YOU JUST CAME IN
ABOUT HEAT—
ME.
HE'S LOOKING HOT THERE . . .
MYSELF.
I HEAR YOUR REQUIREMENTS
ARE FAR MORE THAN YOUR POOR BOILER CAN MEET.
ME.
SHE'S BEING SNIDE NOW . . .
REPORTER.
SHE TELLS ME THEY'VE LAGGED THEIR ATTIC—
MYSELF.
AND ALL OUR CONTROLS ARE THERMOSTATIC, TOO.

Me.
THIS HOUSE IS MY HOUSE . . .
Myself.
AND NOT LIKE YOU.
Me.
CLEAR OUT OF MY HOUSE . . .
Myself.
YOUR HUSBAND TELLS ME
HE'S NOT BEEN WELL.
Me.
OH, HE'S VERY PRONE.
PICKS UP ANYTHING THAT GOES ROUND.
I HOPE YOUR HUSBAND WON'T CATCH IT, TOO.
Myself.
IT DEPENDS HOW STRONG
THEIR RESISTANCE IS.
WHEN MINE CATCHES THINGS,
HE COMES RUNNING BACK HOME
TO ME.
I.
SHE'S GOT YOU THERE, KID . . .
Me.
AND MORE FOOL HE.
I.
YOU'VE GOT HER THERE, KID.
Reporter.
JEAN WAS TELLING ME —
YOU DON'T MIND ME CALLING YOU JEAN?
Me.
OH, SO IT'S JEAN NOW . . .
Reporter.
JEAN HAS JUST BEEN SAYING THAT OUR DECOR
IS THE NICEST SHE'S SEEN.
I.
SHE'S AFTER YOUR HOUSE . . .
Me.
WHAT STRUCK HER AS MOST APPEALING?
I HOPE SHE ADMIRED OUR BEDROOM CEILING, TOO.
I.
THAT BED IS YOUR BED . . .

MYSELF.
A LOVELY BLUE.
I.
SHE'S BEEN IN YOUR BED . . .
MYSELF.
YOUR HUSBAND TELLS ME—
ME.
PLEASE, CALL HIM BILL . . .
MYSELF.
MAY I CALL YOU BILL?
REPORTER.
YES, PLEASE CALL ME BILL.
ME.
JEAN MEET BILL.
MYSELF.
YOUR HUSBAND TELLS ME—
ME.
I'M MARY, PLEASE . . .
MYSELF.
WHAT A PRETTY NAME . . .
ME.
THAT'S THE WAY IT CAME . . .
MYSELF.
SUCH A COMFY NAME . . .
ME.
WELL, IT'S BETTER THAN JOAN OR JEAN . . .
I.
MY NAME IS MY NAME . . .
ME.
I DIDN'T MEAN . . .
I.
OH YES YOU DID, KID.
MYSELF.
I MUST HURRY HOME. TOM WILL WONDER
WHERE I HAVE BEEN.
I.
YOU'VE BEEN IN MY HOUSE.
ME.
YOU COULD ALWAYS TELL HIM . . .
REPORTER.
THANKS FOR POPPING IN AND SEEING US, JEAN.
I.
SHE'S BEEN IN MY BED.

MYSELF.
WHAT WAS IT, NOW, THAT I CAME FOR . . . ?
ME.
HERE'S HOPING ONE DAY I'LL DO THE SAME FOR YOU.
I.
I'LL SLEEP IN HER BED . . .
MYSELF.
I HOPE SO, TOO . . .
I.
SHE SLEPT IN MY BED—
ME.
GIVE TOM MY LOVE, NOW.
MYSELF.
HAVE YOU BOTH MET?
ME.
I RUN INTO HIM
WHEN HE COMES TO DO MODERN DANCE—
REPORTER.
DOES TOM GO DANCING?
ME.
EACH TUESDAY NIGHT.
MYSELF.
SO THAT'S WHERE HE GOES—
REPORTER.
TOMMY TWINKLE-TOES . . .
MYSELF.
I DID NOT SUPPOSE TOM WOULD EVER BEHAVE
LIKE THAT . . .
I.
YOU'VE GOT HER THERE, GIRL . . .
ME.
SO TIT FOR TAT.
I.
CLEAR OUT OF MY HOUSE.
THIS HOUSE IS MY HOUSE.
ME/I.
SO JUST SCRAM.

(*MYSELF is now sitting in ME's chair. REPORTER scribbles.*)

REPORTER. Well, Mary, I don't know how much of that I can
print but . . . Family paper, you know. (*he laughs*)
MYSELF. (*smiling*) Oh, well.

REPORTER. (*studying her slightly puzzledly*) You're—
er . . . You're looking a bit better, anyway. You gave me a
fright a minute ago. Much better.

MYSELF. Yes. I get better when I'm less nervous in myself.

REPORTER. Ah.

MYSELF. Strangers always make me feel clumsy and awkward.
I hate me when I'm like that.

ME. Alright, alright . . .

MYSELF. (*taking REPORTER's glass*) May I?

REPORTER. Yes, help yourself. Sure you wouldn't like me to
—? (*he half rises*)

MYSELF. No, this is fine, thank you. I just needed something to
refresh myself.

ME. She's not going to get us all drunk again, is she?

I. Very probably.

(*They react as MYSELF takes a huge swig from the glass.*)

REPORTER. And how about your own childhood then, Mary?
How would you describe that?

MYSELF. —er . . .

ME. Foul.

I. Awful.

MYSELF. Well . . .

ME. Spoilt.

I. Fat.

MYSELF. Shy, really.

REPORTER. Shy? Oh, that's a nice touch. A shy child.

MYSELF. I suppose it was because I was rather . . .

I. Fat.

MYSELF. Overweight.

REPORTER. Overweight? You mean fat?

MYSELF. —er . . . yes, I suppose . . .

I. Fat.

MYSELF. Fat, yes.

REPORTER. Oh, dear. That made life a bit difficult, I expect,
did it?

MYSELF. A bit.

ME. Impossible.

I. There was this thin girl trying to get out . . .

REPORTER. Especially at dances, I suppose?

MYSELF. (*blankly*) Dances?
REPORTER. You know. Dances.
ME. (*with a shudder*) Dances . . .

[MUSIC #I – 5: *UNLIKELY*]

MYSELF. Oh, yes. Especially at dances.
MYSELF.
THOUGH IT'S NOT LIKELY
I KNOW IT'S UNLIKELY
AS GREAT MIGHT THE LIKELIHOOD BE
OF LIGHTNING STRIKING
AS YOU'D TAKE A LIKING
TO SOMEONE UNLIKELY AS ME . . .
ME/I.
INSIDE THERE'S A FIRE
QUIETLY BLAZING.
COME CLOSER, THE HEAT'S
QUITE AMAZING . . .
ME.
A MAN OF YOUR TASTE
SHOULD SURELY NOW BE ABLE
NOT TO JUDGE THINGS FROM THE LABEL . . .
MYSELF.
IF IT'S MERELY FUN THAT YOU ARE AFTER
YOU CAN GET YOUR SHARE OF LAUGHTER
HERE . . .
ME/I.
SHE IS NOT LIKELY
WE KNOW SHE'S UNLIKELY
ME.
SHE OFTEN LOOKS LIKEWISE TO ME—
ME/I.
PLEASE DON'T BE BLINDED
YOU'RE VERY LIKE-MINDED,
THERE'S NO ONE COULD LOVE YOU LIKE SHE—
MYSELF.
YOU'D BETTER MOVE FAST
I AM WAITING.
IT'S STARTING TO PROVE
SO FRUSTRATING . . .

ME.
REMEMBER THE PHRASE
STILL WATERS RUN MUCH DEEPER?
MYSELF.
I'M WHAT SPY-RINGS CALL A SLEEPER . . .
ME/MYSELF/I.
IF YOU'RE WANTING SOMEONE UNDERCOVER
YOU WILL FIND THE PERFECT LOVER HERE . . .
MYSELF.
THOUGH IT'S UNLIKELY
I KNOW IT'S UNLIKELY
I'D LIKE YOU TO LISTEN TO ME—
LIKELY AS NOT YOU
AS SOON AS I'VE GOT YOU
WILL LIKE HOW OUR LOVING WILL BE . . .
ME/MYSELF/I.
THAT ISN'T UNLIKELY . . .

(*During this last, the REPORTER has got himself another pint.
He sits down beside MYSELF again who still has the re-
mains of his original drink.*)

REPORTER. (*toasting her cheerfully*) Cheers!
MYSELF. (*responding*) Cheers!
ME. (*swallowing with her*) Oh, I do hate beer . . .
REPORTER. Well, never mind. That's all in the past, isn't it?
MYSELF. Right.
REPORTER. You seem to have turned out alright, anyway.
MYSELF. Thank you . . .
I. He makes me sound like a cake . . .
REPORTER. Can't complain now . . .
MYSELF. No . . .
REPORTER. Quite a dish . . .
ME. More of a fruit flan . . .
MYSELF. Well . . . I could say the same . . .
REPORTER. Really?
MYSELF. Yes . . . You're quite a flan yourself . . .
REPORTER. Pardon?
I. Oh, Gawd . . . I wouldn't mind if she chatted them up
properly. She can't even do that . . .
REPORTER. What's a flan?

MYSELF. You are. You're my sort of flan, anyway . . . (*she laughs*)

I. Oh well, that's it, isn't it? She's blown it completely now. There'll be nothing left by the time I get there, that's for sure.

MYSELF. Jolly good beer, isn't it?

REPORTER. Careful, now careful. It's quite strong if you're not used to it. You might live to regret it, eh?

MYSELF. Ooh. The things I've lived to regret. I could tell you . . .

REPORTER. Really?

MYSELF. Ooh-hoo. If I had a mind to . . .

ME. Don't you dare.

REPORTER. Well, watch yourself, Mary. We can't print anything too risque, you know. Can't have our Mum of the Year with an X certificate, can we?

MYSELF. Oh, I'm sorry.

REPORTER. Curse of the Ideal Mummy, eh? (*he laughs*)

(*MYSELF screams with laughter.*)

I. She's away. Hours of subtlety straight down the sink . . .

MYSELF. Oh dear, that's funny. That is funny . . .

ME. Look at her. Look at her . . .

MYSELF. You're a very funny flan . . .

REPORTER. Steady on. You'll have us thrown out in a minute.

I. He's been turned right off.

ME. Not surprised.

MYSELF. Oh, I'm sorry. I don't often go but when I do go I go all at once . . .

REPORTER. That's alright. Nice to see someone enjoying themselves.

ME. Revolting.

I. (*calling to REPORTER*) We do have a nicer side, too, you know. Over here. If you can just hold on, I'll pull myself together . . .

MYSELF. Sorry, I'm drinking all this.

REPORTER. You carry on.

I. Mind you, I'll be flat on my back by the time I get a look in.

ME. As usual.

MYSELF. It's a good job you don't know what really goes on . . .

REPORTER. Where?
MYSELF. On the Nettleford Estate.
REPORTER. What? What goes on?
MYSELF. I wouldn't want to shock you.
REPORTER. No, you won't shock me. It's only the readers that get shocked. Not me. I've seen it all.
MYSELF. All?
REPORTER. Well. Most of it. Come on. What gives on the Nettleford Estate that I don't know about?
MYSELF. Well . . .
ME. She's telling him everything.
MYSELF. You won't be able to print it.
REPORTER. Maybe not but I'd like to hear it.

[MUSIC #I – 6: *THE WIFE-SWAP DANCE*]

I. Well, that's that.
ME. But it's all lies.
I. Some of them . . .
MYSELF. Well . . .
ME. It was nothing to do with me.
I. Oh, yes it was . . .
MYSELF.
STUCK OUT IN SUBURBIA WITH LITTLE TO DO,
WE ARE GRATEFUL FOR THE OFFER OF A
  DIFFERENT VIEW.
ANXIOUS TO TRY ANYTHING THE SLIGHTEST BIT
  NEW,
WE ARE RESTLESSLY EXPLORING
AVENUES LESS BORING
THAN THE ONES THAT WE KNOW—
  I.
NO ONE CAN DENY WE ARE DEVOTED AND TRUE,
  ME.
THOUGH THE ONLY DOUBTFUL QUESTION IS,
  DEVOTED TO WHO?
  MYSELF.
FOR WE, NOT INFREQUENTLY CHANGE PARTNERS
  TOO
  I.
JUST TO TRY AND KEEP OUR REASON,

Me.
MARK A CHANGE OF SEASON . . .
Myself.
OURS IS A SANE ATTITUDE
GLAD TO EMBRACE
SUCH AN INANE PLATITUDE
HOME'S A WOMAN'S PLACE.
I.
PLACING US, STRATEGICALLY, WITH QUITE A
  STRONG VOICE
IN EXPRESSING EVERY PREFERENCE FOR MEN OF
  OUR CHOICE.
Me.
OH, THE WIFE SWAP DANCE
IS A CERTAIN SIGN OF SPRING.
Myself.
MRS. BROWN TURNS GREEN,
I.
GREEN TURNS MERRIWEATHER.
Me/Myself.
ONE BIG CHANCE
FOR THE DOING OF OUR THING,
I.
MRS. GREEN LAST NIGHT
WAKES UP MERRIWEATHER.
Me.
MARITAL UNHAPPINESS HAS LOST ITS MAIN CAUSE.
IF MY HUSBAND GROWS A PROBLEM, THEN
  TOMORROW HE'S YOURS.
Me/Myself/I.
YES, THE WIFE SWAP DANCE
IS A CERTAIN SIGN OF SPRING.
MRS. BROWN TURNS GREEN,
GREEN TURNS MERRIWEATHER.
ONE BIG CHANCE
FOR THE DOING OF OUR THING
MRS. GREEN LAST NIGHT
WAKES UP MERRIWEATHER.
Myself.
IT IS NO COINCIDENCE OUR HOMES ARE THE SAME,
I.
WE ARE ONE BIG HAPPY FAMILY IN ALL BUT

OUR NAME.
  ME.
SCRUPULOUSLY STICKING TO THE RULES OF THE
  GAME,
  MYSELF.
WE MAKE ANYONE CAUGHT CHEATING
LIVE WITH MR. KEATING
AND HIS SMELLY OLD DOG—
  I.
DOGMATISTS HAVE BRANDED US AS WIVES
  WITHOUT SHAME
  ME.
BUT TODAY WE FIND MONOGAMY INCREDIBLY
  TAME.
  MYSELF/I.
IF WE LOOK IDENTICAL, WE'RE HARDLY TO BLAME
  ME.
IT'S THROUGH STRIVING TO LOOK PRETTY
FOR A MALE COMMITTEE.
  MYSELF/I.
IF WE SEEM ONE ENTITY,
LACKING A HEART
WELL, WE FIND NOW MEN TO BE
HARD TO TELL APART.
  ME.
PARTLY WHY WE'RE BUSIER THAN EVER'S BECAUSE
ALL OUR DAYS ARE SPENT IN TRYING TO LEAVE
  THE PLACE AS IT WAS.
  I.
BUT THE WIFE SWAP DANCE
IS A CERTAIN SIGN OF SPRING.
  MYSELF.
MRS. BROWN TURNS GREEN,
  I.
GREEN TURNS MERRIWEATHER.
  ME/MYSELF.
ONE BIG CHANCE
FOR THE DOING OF OUR THING
  I.
MRS. GREEN LAST NIGHT
WAKES UP MERRIWEATHER.

ME.
IF I START COMPARING ALL THOSE HUSBANDS
I'VE HAD,
THEN MY CHOICE OF MAN ORIGINALLY WASN'T
TOO BAD.
ME/MYSELF/I.
HAIL, THE WIFE SWAP DANCE
IT'S A CERTAIN SIGN OF SPRING.
MRS. BROWN TURNS GREEN,
GREEN TURNS MERRIWEATHER.
ONE BIG CHANCE
FOR THE DOING OF OUR THING.
MRS. GREEN LAST NIGHT
WAKES UP MERRIWEATHER.
I.
CALLING US IMMORAL DOESN'T MATTER A DAMN —
ME.
NOW I MUST JUST FIND MY HUSBAND SO I KNOW
WHO I AM . . .

(*I now sits where MYSELF was, by the REPORTER.*)

REPORTER. (*after a pause*) Do you know, it's my greatest regret
that I've never lived anywhere where they do that sort of thing.
I've always missed out on that. Wife swapping.
I. (*sympathetically*) Are you married?
REPORTER. No. (*pause*) Ah. See what you mean. I hadn't
looked at it that way . . .
MYSELF. Either I'm getting brighter or he's getting more
stupid.
REPORTER. Well, Mary, I'll probably be able to sell the film
rights of this story but I don't think, quite frankly, we're going to
get it past Mr. Ash.
I. Maybe that's as well.
REPORTER. I haven't really got a lot down here I can use.
(*smiling at her*) Anyway, it's ridiculous. You know something?
You look much too young to be Mum of the Year. Quite
ridiculous.
I. Thank you . . . (*she lowers her eyes demurely*)
REPORTER. No, really. You look smashing. You really do.
You're like . . . you're like . . .

MYSELF. Steak and Kidney Pudding . . .

ME. Shhh!

I. Ssh!

REPORTER. Sorry. Am I saying the wrong thing?

I. No. Carry on. I wasn't shushing you.

REPORTER. No?

I. No.

REPORTER. Ah . . .

I. You were saying I'm like . . .

REPORTER. —Er . . . yes . . . you're . . .

MYSELF. Get on with it!

REPORTER. Well, don't take this the wrong way, will you —?

ME. Yes.

MYSELF. Probably.

REPORTER. You've got one of those faces that grows on you, you know.

I. Thank you.

ME. What the hell's that supposed to mean?

MYSELF. Terrific.

REPORTER. It's a face that glows, you know.

MYSELF. All the make-up's worn off, that's why.

ME. She's shining like a beacon . . .

REPORTER. Lovely. (*he gazes into I's eyes*)

MYSELF. Couple of glasses of beer and he's anybody's.

ME. Couple of glasses of beer and you're nobody's.

REPORTER. You say your husband's in electronics?

I. That's right.

REPORTER. Is he a traveller or —?

I. He travels a bit.

MYSELF. Oy-oy . . .

REPORTER. Ah.

I. Now and then.

ME. What's she doing?

MYSELF. Guess.

REPORTER. Well . . . if you're ever at a . . . you know . . .

MYSELF. . . . loose . . .

REPORTER. . . . loose . . .

ME. . . . end . . .

REPORTER. . . . end . . . you know . . .

I. Sometimes.

REPORTER. Well . . .

I. What?

ME. Oh, it embarrasses me so much when I behave like this . . .

REPORTER. Enough said.

I. Right. Say no more.

ME. It's so blazen . . .

MYSELF. Brazen.

ME. I mean brazen.

I. You know where I live.

REPORTER. Yes. (*consulting his notebook*) It's Somewhereor-other Gardens, isn't it—er . . . Have you got a phone?

I. Yes we have. We're very lucky.

REPORTER. Ah.

[MUSIC #1–7: *OPEN FOR LOVE*]

I.

THE ATMOSPHERE'S HARDLY RIGHT,
THERE ISN'T A STAR IN SIGHT,
BUT NEVERTHELESS I MIGHT
BE OPEN FOR LOVE . . .

THERE ISN'T A HARVEST MOON
THIS TIME OF THE AFTERNOON.
IT REALLY IS FAR TOO SOON
TO OPEN FOR LOVE.
BUT IF YOUR REQUIREMENT
IS TERRIBLY URGENT,
I'LL MAKE AN EXCEPTION
AND OPEN THE STORE.
I NEVER LIKE KEEPING
A CUSTOMER WAITING
I'LL ROLL UP THE SHUTTERS,
UNFASTEN THE OLD FRONT DOOR . . .

I'M USUALLY CLOSED TODAY,
RE-DOING THE MAIN DISPLAY,
BUT SEEING IT'S YOU, I MAY
JUST OPEN FOR LOVE.

WHATEVER YOUR NEEDS ENTAIL,

I WELCOME THE SMALLEST SALE,
I'VE NEVER BEEN KNOW TO FAIL
TO OPEN FOR LOVE.

I SAW YOU THERE LOOKING
YOUR NOSE AT THE WINDOW,
LIKE SOME HUNGRY SCHOOLBOY,
YOUR EYES BIG AND WIDE.
WELL, LET ME ASSURE YOU
THE WINDOW'S ALL DRESSING.
YOU'VE REALLY SEEN NOTHING
TILL YOU'VE HAD A LOOK INSIDE . . .
    ME/MYSELF.
STEP IN AND AVOID THE COLD.
WE WELCOME YOU, YOUNG AND OLD.
WE'VE NEVER YET UNDERSOLD
WHEN OPEN FOR LOVE.
    I.
AND SINCE MY REQUIREMENT
IS TERRIBLY URGENT,
I'LL MAKE AN EXCEPTION
AND OPEN THE STORE . . .
    ME/MYSELF.
WE NEVER LIKE KEEPING
A CUSTOMER WAITING
WE'LL ROLL UP THE SHUTTERS,
UNFASTEN THE OLD FRONT DOOR . . .
    ME/MYSELF/I.
IT'S NEARER TO NOON THAN NIGHT,
THIS LIGHTING IS FAR TOO BRIGHT
BUT SOMEHOW THE TIMES ARE RIGHT
TO OPEN FOR LOVE.
OPEN FOR LOVE . . .

(*REPORTER and I, sitting as before.*)

REPORTER. (*rather unnerved*) Well, what can I say,
Mary . . . ? (*he laughs nervously*)
MYSELF. Panic.
ME. He's panicking . . .
MYSELF. We've panicked him.
REPORTER. Yes, well, that all makes good . . . Oh, my

heavens . . . Look at that. Look at the time. It's nearly—Oh dear. I've got to be dashing off, Mary.

I. Are you sure?

REPORTER. Sorry.

ME. Rats . . .

MYSELF. Rats . . .

I. Rats . . .

REPORTER. Rats?

I. Rats that, then.

REPORTER. C'est la vie.

I. What a shame.

ME. Blazen. She's so blazen.

MYSELF. Brazen.

I. (*calling after him as he goes*) 20662.

REPORTER. Eh?

ME. We used to say blazen when we were little, didn't we?

MYSELF. Well, we're big girls now.

I. 20662. My phone number.

REPORTER. Oh, yes. Yes, of course. Thank you. (*he makes to scribble it down*)

MYSELF. 20662?

ME. That's Enid Merriweather's number.

I. 24 Caldicott Gardens . . . Have you got that?

ME. 24?

MYSELF. Mr. Keating's place . . .

ME. He'll never get past the dog . . .

REPORTER. Right. Bye, then.

I. Bye, bye. (*calling after him*) By the way . . .

REPORTER. (*turning back somewhat reluctantly*) Yes?

I. (*loudly*) My husband's always away on Tuesdays and Thursdays.

REPORTER. (*looking round nervously*) Ah. Good . . .

I. So you know what to do, eh?

REPORTER. Right, right . . .

I. Any time you fancy a slice of flan, eh? (*she winks*)

REPORTER. (*laughing somewhat hysterically*) Yes. Yes. (*as he goes, to himself*) My God!

(*He hurries out. The women watch him go.*)

ME. (*smiling despite herself*) Blazen.

ME/MYSELF/I. (*together, as one woman*) Ha!

[MUSIC #1-8: *ME, MYSELF AND I*]

REPORTER.
CAN YOU TELL US WHY YOUR MARRIAGE HAS
    ENDED—?
WHAT ABOUT THIS GREEK YOU'VE LATELY
    BEFRIENDED—?
IS IT REALLY TRUE YOUR HEART NEVER MENDED—?
HOW ABOUT THE PRIEST YOU SAY YOU'VE
    OFFENDED—?
I.
YOU ASK THE QUESTIONS—
I WILL REPLY.
ALWAYS PROVIDING
YOU LET ME TALK
ABOUT
ME, MYSELF AND I . . .
I'LL REVEAL
ALL THOSE LOVERS THERE'VE BEEN,
HOW I ONCE SNUBBED THE QUEEN,
HOW I POSED FOR
PABLO . . .
REPORTER.
WILL YOU DARE DENY THE RUMOURS THEY'RE
    SPREADING—?
IS IT REALLY TRUE YOU STREAKED AT YOUR
    WEDDING—?
DO YOU STILL REGARD YOUR HUSBANDS AS
    BEDDING—?
HOW IS YOUR CAREER AND WHERE IS IT HEADING—?
ME.
ME, I'LL BE HONEST,
BRUTALLY FRANK.
ME, I CAN TELL IT
JUST AS IT WAS,
THE TRUTH—
ME, MYSELF AND I.
NOW READ ON:—
FOR THAT LIST OF M.P.S.
I COULD BRING TO THEIR KNEES

FOR MY NIGHTS WITH

ENGLAND'S
TEST TEAM—
THE HIGHEST SOME OF THEM SCORED FOR
  SEVERAL SEASONS—
FOR ALL THEIR AVERAGES
UP UNTIL TEA
READ IT IN ME,
MYSELF AND I.
  REPORTER.
DID YOUR FATHER DRINK AND DID HE MISTREAT
  YOU—?
IS IT TRUE YOU SWORE WHEN THE POPE
  WOULDN'T MEET YOU—?
DID YOU LEAVE THE SHEIKH THE DAY THAT HE
  BEAT YOU—?
DO YOU EVER FEEL THAT AGE WILL DEFEAT YOU—?
  MYSELF.
NOW IS MY CHANCE TO
SPEAK FOR MYSELF.
TELL OF MY CHILDHOOD,
BORN IN A SLUM.
PART ONE.
ME, MYSELF AND I.
HOW MY DAD
SENT ME OUT ON THE GAME,
HOW MY MUM DIED OF SHAME.
HOW MY LIFE'S BEEN
ONE LONG
LONGING,
FOR LOVE OF MERELY MYSELF AND NOT MY BODY.
SO GET YOUR COPY NOW,
TURN TO PAGE THREE,
READ ABOUT ME, MYSELF AND I.
  REPORTER.
HOW CAN YOU WEAR MINK AND PREACH
  CONSERVATION—?
DO YOU EVER DRESS FOR SHEER TITILLATION—?
DID YOU WRITE DOWN WHORE AS CHIEF
  OCCUPATION—?
DID THE MARRIAGE END WITHOUT
  CONSUMMATION—?

I.
I AM THE SUBJECT
I WILL TELL ALL,
HOW A SEX OBJECT
TOOK ON THE WORLD.
HERE COME
  ME/MYSELF/I.
ME, MYSELF AND I.
WE'LL RECALL
ALL THE HUSBANDS WE'VE HAD,
HOW EACH MARRIAGE WENT BAD,
HOW WE SUED OUR
PLASTIC
SURGEONS.
THE SECRET STORY OF HOW WE HAD OUR BABY.
IT'S THE ONE THE WORLD'S
WAITING TO SEE.
ALL ABOUT ME,
MYSELF AND I.

END OF ACT ONE

ACT II

[MUSIC #II – 1(a): *RECITATIVE II*]

ME.
INTRODUCING
MRS. M. YATELY,
MOTHER OF FOUR
(NO A LEVELS)
OF FOURTEEN CALDICOTT GARDENS,
NETTLEFORD ESTATE,
EAST HOPLEY,
NEAR NETTLEFORD,
NORTH YORKS.
(WITH A POSTCODE I CAN NEVER REMEMBER)
ABOUT TO BE INTERVIEWED BY:—
MR. RODNEY BIRCH OF THE EVENING PAPER
(OR IT MIGHT BE MR. ASH)
BECAUSE I'VE WON THE IDEAL MUM COMPETITION,
ORGANISED BY THE EVENING ECHO—
WHICH I DIDN'T GO IN FOR.
IT WAS OUR MARJORIE—
THE SORT OF INTERVIEW
THAT COULD MAKE ME A NATIONAL STAR
OVERNIGHT.
MYSELF.
MYSELF
ME.
WHY ME?
MYSELF.
HE'LL HAVE WRITTEN IT BEFORE HE GETS HERE—
I.
WHAT DO I SAY TO HIM?
ME.
MY SECRET IS THAT I AM BLESSED
WITH A WONDERFUL HUSBAND
AND FOUR WONDERFUL CHILDREN
MYSELF.
HA!
ME.
ADMITTED MRS. MARY

41

MYSELF.
SUSAN
I.
LESLEY
ME.
YATELY,
MYSELF.
ATTRACTIVE
I.
DYED
ME.
BRUNETTE.
I.
AGED THIRTY-FOUR,
MYSELF.
FIVE
ME.
TOLD ME WITH A SMILE
MYSELF/I.
A SMILE . . .
ME.
WHY DOES IT MAKE ME SOUND SO BORING?
MYSELF.
BECAUSE YOU ARE BORING.
I.
NOT TRUE—
ME.
MIND YOU, MY FRIENDS HAVE SOMETIMES SAID
THERE'S MORE TO YOU
THAN MEETS THE EYE, MARY.
HUSBAND.
MARY—
ME.
OH, YES—
MYSELF/I.
OH, YES—
HUSBAND.
MARY—
ME.
I'M ABSOLUTELY CERTAIN
MYSELF.
OH, YES

I.
OH, YES
HUSBAND.
MARY, WHAT THE HELL ARE YOU DOING THERE?
I. (*seeing him*)
OH, NO—
MYSELF. (*seeing him*)
OH, NO—
ME. (*seeing him*)
OH, NO—
HUSBAND.
MARY—
ME.
HALLO.
HUSBAND.
ARE YOU ALRIGHT, MARY?
I.
YES,
MYSELF.
NO.
ME.
PERFECTLY—

[MUSIC #II–1(b): *NO MORE*]

I'LL HAVE NO MORE
SITTING AT HOME—
THERE IS MUCH MORE TO LIFE
THERE IS MUCH MORE TO SEE
THAN A SINK.
I WANT NO MORE
WASHING FOR SIX
THERE IS MORE TO ME
    ME/MYSELF/I.
THERE IS MUCH MORE TO US
THAN YOU THINK.
    ME.
READ THE DETAILS IN YOUR PAPER
ALL ABOUT THIS GREAT ESCAPER—
WINNER OF
MUM OF THE
YEAR IS NOW FREE—

ME/MYSELF/I.
EVENING ECHO'S
OUTRIGHT WINNER
LARGE CASH PRIZES
GALA DINNER
THRILLING PICTURES
ALL BEGINNING TODAY . . .
HUSBAND.
MARY, YOU'VE BEEN
UNDER TENSION
THERE IS SOME MIS—
APPREHENSION
NOWHERE DOES THE
PAPER MENTION YOUR NAME—

YOU HAVE NOT WON
MUM OF THE YEAR
YOU HAVE LEFT THE KIDS
THANK THE LORD MRS. BROWN
WAS AROUND.
I HAVE LEFT MY
MEETING AT WORK
JUST TO TRACK YOU DOWN,
WORRIED TO DEATH UNTIL
YOU WERE FOUND—

I PUT TWO AND TWO TOGETHER
THANKS TO ENID MERRIWEATHER—
THINKING YOU'RE
MUM OF THE
YEAR IS ABSURD.
ME.
I'VE NOT WON IT?
HUSBAND.
WELL, HOW COULD YOU?
ME.
MARJIE TOLD ME—
HUSBAND.
WELL, SHE WOULD DO—
WINNING THAT WOULD
NOT BE GOOD FOR MY JOB—
ME.
I AM MEETING

THIS REPORTER . . .
HUSBAND.
WOULD YOU LIKE A
GLASS OF WATER?
YOU LOOK TIRED
AND OVERWROUGHT, YOU OLD THING.

THERE'LL BE NO MORE
MUM OF THE YEAR.
I HAVE HEARD ENOUGH
GATHER UP ALL YOUR STUFF
AND COME HOME.

(*At the end, ME is seated. HUSBAND stands.*) Mary?

ME. (*dreamily*) Mmm?
HUSBAND. Are you coming?
ME. Mmm?
HUSBAND. Home? Are you coming home?
ME. Alright . . .
I. No—
MYSELF. No—
ME. No.
HUSBAND. What?
ME. In a minute . . .
MYSELF. In an hour . . .
I. In a week . . .
HUSBAND. I'll get you a drink. What would you like? A squash?
Want a squash? Is that what you'd like? Orange squash?
I. Gin.
MYSELF. Creme de Menthe and Tequila . . .
ME. Yes. Orange squash, please . . .
MYSELF. Yuk.
HUSBAND. (*moving away*) I'll fetch you one. Wait there.
(*stopping momentarily*) I mean, I was in a very important meet-
ing, Mary. Very important indeed. We are talking about a million
and a quarter pounds worth of electronics. That's what was at
stake . . . And I have to rush out in the middle, chasing after my
wife. I don't know what the Arabs must have thought . . .
I. They have so many wives they probably wouldn't miss
one . . .
HUSBAND. So . . .
ME. Sorry.
HUSBAND. Wait there. (*he goes to the bar*)

[MUSIC #II – 2: *ELECTRIC WOMAN*]

ME.
I HAVE A HUSBAND IN ELECTRONIC ENGINEERING
HE'S IN A WORLD THAT'S SO TINY IT IS
    DISAPPEARING.
HE'D WED A CIRCUIT
IF HE COULD WORK IT —
HE ONLY LOVES THE SMALL.
I HARDLY EAT AT ALL.

IF YOU ARE MARRIED TO ELECTRONIC ENGINEERING
IT'S NOT THE WOMEN BUT FLOPPY DISCS
YOU FIND YOU'RE FEARING
NOT BY YOUR SISTER
BY A TRANSISTOR
YOU'LL BE AT LAST REPLACED.
SOMEONE COMPUTER BASED.

WHEN ELECTRIC WOMAN
IS PERFECTED
WHEN ELECTRIC WOMAN
IS CONNECTED —
SEE ELECTRIC WOMAN
TURN MY HUSBAND ON —

I'LL BE REJECTED.

WHEN ELECTRIC WOMAN
IS REPLACING
PRE-ELECTRIC WOMAN
(SAVE THE CASING)
NON-ELECTRIC WOMAN
WILL BE DEAD AND GONE —

LYING NEGLECTED.

ALTHOUGH MY HUSBAND'S IN ELECTRONIC
    ENGINEERING
I KNOW IT'S PROTO-TYPE WOMEN THAT HE'S
    PIONEERING.
HE WILL RETURN ME,

DUMP ME AND BURN ME
SOON AS THE DAY ARRIVES—LOGICALLY
PROCESSED WIVES.

WHEN YOU ARE MARRIED TO ELECTRONIC
    ENGINEERING
YOU ARE AWARE THAT SUCH PROSPECTS
COULD BE SHORTLY NEARING,
ONCE HE WAS SEXY,
NOW HE JUST CHECKS ME
ON HIS OSCILLOSCOPE—
NONE OF US HAS A HOPE.

WHEN ELECTRIC WOMAN
IS PERFECTED,
WHEN ELECTRIC WOMAN'S
FIRST CONNECTED,
WATCH ELECTRIC WOMAN
TRIP MY HUSBAND'S SWITCH—

HE'LL BE IGNITED.
    CHORUS.
HAIL, ELECTRIC WOMAN
    ME.
WELCOME, LADIES—
    CHORUS.
HI, ELECTRIC WOMAN
    ME.
MICRO-BABIES
    CHORUS.
SWEET, ELECTRIC WOMAN
    ME.
INTEGRATED BITCH—

YOU WEREN'T INVITED.

WOMEN, THE ENEMY'S ELECTRONIC ENGINEERING.
THIS IS THE CAUSE FOR WHICH
WE SHOULD ALL BE VOLUNTEERING,
CHECK IN YOUR BASEMENT
FOR YOUR REPLACEMENT—
HAS HE MADE PLANS TO WED

SOMETHING THAT'S IN HIS SHED?

IS ELECTRIC WOMAN
SOMEWHERE LURKING?
WILL ELECTRIC WOMAN
SOON BE WORKING?
HAS ELECTRIC WOMAN
WON YOUR HUSBAND'S SOUL

WITH HER INSISTANCE—?
   CHORUS.
CAN ELECTRIC WOMAN
   ME.
MAKE HIM HAPPY?
   CHORUS.
CAN ELECTRIC WOMAN
   ME.
CHANGE A NAPPY?
   CHORUS.
WILL ELECTRIC WOMAN
   ME.
EVER FIT THE ROLE?

CHECK YOUR RESISTANCE—

WE'LL BE THE VICTIMS OF ELECTRONIC
   ENGINEERING
IF WE DON'T MOBILISE,
START SOME ACTIVE INTERFERING.
I HAVE INSISTED
WE SHOULD BE LISTED
WOMEN NOT MICRO-CHIPS
SHOULD BE ON ALL OUR LIPS—
   CHORUS.
SOON ELECTRIC WOMAN
   ME.
WILL BE COURTED.
   CHORUS.
CHEAP ELECTRIC WOMAN
   I.
ALL-IMPORTED

CHORUS.
IF ELECTRIC WOMAN
MYSELF/I.
ISN'T SHORTED OUT.
ME.
REACH FOR YOUR LASER—
CHORUS.
JAM ELECTRIC WOMAN
MYSELF/I.
AND CONFUSE HER
CHORUS.
EARTH ELECTRIC WOMAN
ME.
TRY TO FUSE HER
CHORUS.
TILL ELECTRIC WOMAN
ME/MYSELF/I.
OVERLOADS THROUGHOUT.
I.
THAT OUGHT TO PHASE HER—
ME.
THANKS TO MY HUSBAND IN ELECTRONIC
    ENGINEERING
IF I'M DISTURBED AT ALL,
HE IS THERE TO FIX MY GEARING,
HOW LONG HE'LL TEND ME
SERVICE AND MEND ME
WILL ALL DEPEND. THE
DAY HE'LL EXPEND ME,
HE WILL JUST END ME
SWITCH MY ELECTRIC OFF.

(*At the end of this, ME, MYSELF and I have all frozen in odd
    positions. HUSBAND returns with a glass of orange squash.*)

HUSBAND. What's the matter?
ME. What?
HUSBAND. Why are you sitting like that?
ME. How do you mean?
HUSBAND. In that extraordinary position? Have you done
something to yourself?

I. Yes.

MYSELF. Probably . . .

ME. No.

HUSBAND. (*handing her the orange squash*) There you are.

ME. Thank you. Aren't you having one?

HUSBAND. An orange squash?

ME. A drink?

HUSBAND. Not with the Arabs—

ME. Oh . . .

HUSBAND. They wouldn't like it. Not if they smelt it. Could damage the deal.

ME. Oh. (*she drinks*)

(*MYSELF and I also drink.*)

MYSELF. Ugh! Why do we always have to drink orange squash?

I. For old time's sake . . .

MYSELF. How do you mean?

I. Don't you remember? Orange squash . . .

MYSELF. Orange squash . . . ? Oh, yes. *Orange squash* . . .

HUSBAND. That alright?

ME. Yes, I was . . .

HUSBAND. What?

ME. Remembering.

HUSBAND. Rembering what? Mary, you really are in the most peculiar state . . .

ME. Remembering when I first drank orange squash . . .

HUSBAND. How can you? You were probably only six months old.

ME. No, I meant when we met. You and I. I was drinking orange squash then.

HUSBAND. Good Lord. Really? You can remember that?

ME. Oh, yes. At the dance.

HUSBAND. Dance?

ME. In the village hall. The East Hopley village hall. The church social.

HUSBAND. Oh, my God, yes. The church social . . .

[MUSIC #II–3: *CLOSER*]

I.

HE'S GETTING MUCH CLOSER,

SO VERY MUCH CLOSER.
HE'S LOOKING THIS WAY NOW —
EYES DOWN —
HE'S EVER SO CLOSE NOW.
HE'S LIFTING AN EYEBROW.
NOW HE MUST HAVE SEEN ME SURELY.

OH GOD!
HOW LONG CAN I SIT DEMURELY?
HERE, ON THE EDGE OF MY FIRST AFFAIR,
SWATHED IN PINK CHIFFON WITH SHOULDERS BARE.
I'M SO SURE,
DEEP IN MY TEENAGE HEART,
MY ROMANCE
COULD BE ABOUT TO START
IF ONLY . . .
HE'D GET A BIT CLOSER.
I'M WILLING HIM CLOSER . . .
   HUSBAND.
I'M MOVING IN CLOSER.
SO SUBTLY CLOSER.
SHE'S SITTING ALONE THERE,
EYES DOWN.
I'M HOPING SHE NOTICED
MY TRICK WITH THE EYEBROW.
OR IS SHE ONE MORE DISSEMBLING
WOMAN?
HAPPY JUST TO KEEP ME TREMBLING
HERE, ON THE EDGE OF MY FIRST AFFAIR,
STEEPED IN VALDERMA WITH BRYLCREAMED HAIR.
I'M SO SURE,
DEEP IN MY TEENAGE HEART,
MY ROMANCE
COULD BE ABOUT TO START
IF ONLY . . .
SHE'D BOTHER TO NOTICE
ME GETTING MUCH CLOSER.
   I.
I'D BETTER NOT NOTICE
HIM GETTING MUCH CLOSER . . .
   HUSBAND.
SO CLOSE I COULD TOUCH HER . . .

I.
TOUCH ME . . .
HUSBAND.
HER SKIN IS LIKE PEACHES . . .
I.
I HOPE HE WON'T SEE THAT
BRUISE I GOT IN NETBALL PRACTICE . . .
HUSBAND.
TURN ROUND—
FOR THE UNDISPUTED FACT IS
I/HUSBAND.
WE'RE ON THE EDGE OF OUR FIRST AFFAIR—
ONCE WE ACKNOWLEDGE THE OTHER'S THERE.
WE'RE SO SURE,
DEEP IN OUR TEENAGE HEARTS,
OUR ROMANCE
COULD BE ABOUT TO START
IF ONLY—
I.
HE'D GET A BIT CLOSER . . .
HUSBAND.
THE SMELL OF HER PERFUME—
I.
HE SMELLS OF VALDERMA.
I/HUSBAND.
WE'RE PRACTICALLY CLOSE ENOUGH
HUSBAND.
INCHES FROM BLISS.
I.
CLOSER LIKE THIS.
I/HUSBAND.
CLOSE AS A KISS . . .

(*HUSBAND and ME, as before.*)

HUSBAND. (*after a pause*) We'd better be off. I have to get back.
ME. (*drinking some more*) Oh, yes . . .
HUSBAND. Fancy you remembering that . . .
ME. Well . . .
MYSELF. He doesn't remember anything.
HUSBAND. I'd forgotten all about that.

MYSELF. He bought me a brooch with my name on it so he could recognize me in a crowd . . .

I. Why can't he remember if I do?

MYSELF. If my wife is in the room would she please put her hand up so I can identify her . . . Thank you.

ME. Sssh!

HUSBAND. What?

ME. Oh, nothing.

HUSBAND. You've been doing a lot of that lately.

ME. What?

HUSBAND. Talking to yourself.

ME. Oh. (*she rises to leave*)

I. It's the only conversation we get. Some of us.

MYSELF. Too right. Handbag—!

I. Handbag—!

ME. Oh! My handbag . . .

HUSBAND. O.K. I'll get it. (*as he gets it*) Look, I'll tell you what. I'll ask Peggy Brown if she'd mind keeping the kids for the afternoon, shall I? Then you can take things quietly. Put your feet up for an hour or two. How about that?

ME. No, it's alright . . .

HUSBAND. Well, all this Mum of the Year Competition business. You're obviously in a bit of a state. What on earth gave you the idea you'd won a thing like that?

ME. I don't know . . . I've forgotten.

MYSELF. Because we're all going round the bend, that's why.

I. Shhh! Don't set her off again.

ME. Anyway, I'm going out this evening.

HUSBAND. Are you?

MYSELF. Are we?

I. Are we?

ME. To my dance class . . .

MYSELF/I. Oh, no!

HUSBAND. Oh, come on. Can't you skip that?

ME. I enjoy them.

HUSBAND. Complete and utter waste of time. I mean, if you're going to do night classes, why don't you do something useful? Like pottery?

ME. I don't like pottery.

HUSBAND. Well, at least it's useful.

MYSELF. We don't like pottery . . .

I. We hate pottery . . .
HUSBAND. A few nice pots . . .
MYSELF. We have enough pottery at home, thank you very much.
HUSBAND. . . . lovely . . .
I. . . . which we spend our life washing up . . .
HUSBAND. . . . why not?
ME. (*vehemently*) Because I loathe and detest pottery!
HUSBAND. (*surprised, soothing her*) Alright, alright. Easy. Easy there . . .
I. He thinks I'm a bloody horse . . .
HUSBAND. Easy . . . (*MYSELF and I whinny. After a pause*) It's all getting you just a bit down, isn't it?
ME. (*faintly*) Down?
HUSBAND. The kids. The house. Me. Everything.
I. God. At times he can be shrewd.
MYSELF. His gimlet eyes narrowed and bored into her very soul.
ME. (*still finishing her drink*) Sorry, I won't be a minute.
HUSBAND. It's alright. Take your time.
MYSELF. Take your time? What does he mean—take your time? He's done nothing but chase us . . .
ME. Alright. Alright.
HUSBAND. Yes. Alright, take it easy . . .
I. Whoa there, girl!
HUSBAND. They'll have adjourned, anyway. The meeting. For lunch. (*sudden thought*) I'll have missed the lunch.
ME. Oh.

[MUSIC #II–4: *TEACHING THE CHILDREN*]

HUSBAND. That's a pity . . .
I. Oh dear, oh dear, oh dear . . .
MYSELF.
LISTEN WITH MOTHER WAS LOVELY TODAY,
ALL ABOUT TEDDY WHO LOOKED IN TO PLAY.
SHARON ENJOYED IT, AND SUSIE AND FAY.
TIMMY WAS SLEEPING UPSTAIRS.

WE'VE BEEN HERE
JUST THE KIDS AND ME,

SEEN NO ONE ELSE FOR A WEEK.

I HAVE SPENT
EVERY HOUR I CAN,
TEACHING THE CHILDREN TO SPEAK.

SHARON IS READING OUT JANET AND JOHN.
JANET IS CRY—ING THEIR PUS—SY CAT'S GONE.
SUSIE AND FAY ARE BOTH SOLDIERING ON—
TIMMY IS SLEEPING UPSTAIRS.

BILL'S GONE OFF ON A BUSINESS TRIP
SOMEWHERE IN SOUTH MARTINIQUE.

WE AGREED
IT WAS BOTH OUR JOBS,
TEACHING THE CHILDREN TO SPEAK.

SUSIE, WHEN READING, HAS TROUBLE WITH D'S.
SHARON CAN'T RECOGNISE C's FROM HER G's.
FAY STILL SAYS CHUFF-CHUFF AND WIZZ-WIZZ
   FOR WEES.
TIMMY GOES BYE-BYES UPSTAIRS.

WE BEEN HERE
JUS' THE KIDS N' ME
TIM-TIM'S NEW BUN-BUN WON' SQUEAK.
MAMA HERE
EVERY WEENY HOUR
TEACHY GOO-GUM-GUMS GOO-WEEK . . .

(HUSBAND and ME as before. Under the next, HUSBAND
   dozes off.)

[MUSIC #II – 5(a): RECITATIVE III]

   ME.
I THINK THE MAJOR PROBLEM LIES WITH ME . . .
   I.
I DON'T THINK SO . . .
   MYSELF.
I AGREE.

I.
WITH ME?
MYSELF.
WITH HER.
ME.
WITH ME.
IF ONLY, BILL, WE COULD JUST ONCE OR TWICE
SIT DOWN AND TALK . . .
MYSELF.
HEAR, HEAR . . .
ME.
INSTEAD OF MERELY PASSING INFORMATION . . .
MYSELF.
YOUR LIGHT GREEN SOCKS ARE IN THE WASH—
I.
AND SHARON'S LOST HER THIRD LEFT GYM
SHOE . . .
ME.
AND WHEN YOU HAVE LUNCH OUT
AVOID STEAK PIE AND APPLE CRUMBLE,
THAT WE HAVE TONIGHT . . .
I.
THE BEDROOM WINDOW'S STUCK AGAIN . . .
MYSELF.
THE BATHROOM LIGHT HAS GONE AND I CAN'T
REACH . . .
ME.
IT'S ALL SO TRIVIAL!
I WISH THAT ONCE, JUST ONCE
WE COULD . . .
MYSELF.
OH, SAVE YOUR BREATH,
HE'S ASLEEP AGAIN . . .
I.
I'M NOT SURPRISED . . .

[MUSIC #II–5(b): *WHERE?*]

ME.
WHERE IS THE MAN THAT I MARRIED
THOSE YEARS AGO?
I WONDER

WHO IS THIS SOMNOLENT STRANGER
I HARDLY KNOW?
OR TELL ME
COULD IT BE ME—
   I.
SHOULDN'T I ASK THE QUESTION
   MYSELF.
HAVE I MYSELF TO—?
   I.
WHERE IS THE MAN WHO APPLAUDED
EACH WORD I SAID?
WHAT HAPPENED?
IS HE THE MAN WHO NOW WATCHES
CROSSROADS INSTEAD?
OR MAYBE—
   ME.
MAYBE IT'S ME.
   I.
SHOULDN'T I ASK THE QUESTION
   MYSELF.
HAVE I MYSELF TO BLAME?
   ME.
BUT IT'S FUNNY HOW SOME MEMORIES
JUST RETURN.
DO THEY CARRY ANY LESSONS
THAT WE COULD LEARN?
   MYSELF/I.
NO, THIS ISN'T THE MAN THAT WE MARRIED
I'M SURE OF THAT
THERE'S A MISTAKE.
   ME.
I'M REMEMBERING AN EVENING
IN THE RAIN.
WILL I EVER SEE HIM LAUGHING
LIKE THAT AGAIN?
   MYSELF/I.
BUT YOU'RE HARDLY THE WOMAN HE MARRIED,
LET US BE FAIR
QUESTIONING—
   I.
WHERE IS THE HERO I WORSHIPPED?
THOUGHT I WOULD DIE . . .

MYSELF.
WHERE IS HE?
ME.
EACH TIME HE WHISPERED HE LOVED ME,
I USED TO CRY.
THAT REALLY
CAN'T HAVE BEEN ME . . .
I.
SHOULDN'T I ASK THE QUESTION
MYSELF.
HAVE I MYSELF TO BLAME?
I.
I'M REMEMBERING A MOMENT
WE WERE OUT—
WHEN OUR LOVE BECAME TOO URGENT
TO HANG ABOUT . . .
ME/MYSELF.
YOU'RE NO LONGER A WOMAN OF TWENTY
LET'S FACE THE FACTS
QUERYING—
I.
WHERE'S THE MOST BRILLIANT LOVER
NATURE'S DEVISED?
MYSELF.
GOD HELP ME!
NOW IF I MENTION THE SUBJECT
HE LOOKS SURPRISED—
ME.
I GUESS IT'S
PROBABLY ME . . .
I.
SHOULDN'T I ASK THE QUESTION
MYSELF.
HAVE I MYSELF TO BLAME?
ME/MYSELF/I.
BUT IT'S FUNNY HOW SOME MEMORIES
JUST RETURN.
DO THEY CARRY ANY LESSONS
THAT WE COULD LEARN?
MYSELF/I.
FOR IT'S NORMAL FOR PEOPLE TO ALTER
THAT YOU EXPECT.
NEVERTHELESS . . .

ME.
COULD IT BE ME?
MYSELF.
IS IT MYSELF?
I.
MAYBE IT'S I . . .
ME/MYSELF/I.
COULD IT BE US?

(*ME with HUSBAND who is still asleep.*)

ME. (*waking him gently*) Bill. . . . Bill. . . .
HUSBAND. (*starting awake*) Wha—?
ME. Wake up . . .
HUSBAND. Was I asleep then? Did I doze off . . . ?
ME. Yes.
HUSBAND. I didn't doze off, did I?
ME. You did.
MYSELF. Yes.
HUSBAND. My God. I've never done that, have I? Dozed off?
I've never done that before.
I. He's always doing that . . .
HUSBAND. You know, I must be more exhausted than I rea-
lised. Extraordinary. Were people staring?
ME. What at?
HUSBAND. At me? Dozing off?
ME. I don't think so.
MYSELF. Probably got better things to stare at . . .
HUSBAND. I must be totally drained. Mustn't I? Eh?
ME. (*rising*) Right. I've finished. Are you coming then?
HUSBAND. Just a minute . . .
ME. I thought you were in a hurry . . .
HUSBAND. Just sit down. For a minute. Please.
MYSELF. What's he up to? He only says please at Christmas
when his mother's here . . .
ME. What?
HUSBAND. (*searching for words*) Look . . .
I. He's probably going to give us a lecture . . .
HUSBAND. It's just . . . well . . .
MYSELF. Now, Mary, if *you* don't remember to switch off the
lavatory lights how can you expect the children to switch off the
lavatory lights . . . ?
ME. Well?

HUSBAND. Nothing. I just thought we'd . . .

MYSELF. What's the point of having the central heating blazing away if you go and leave the back door open . . .

I. Shh!

MYSELF. What?

HUSBAND. It's just . . . (*he pauses*)

I. I think he's trying to tell us something . . .

ME. What?

HUSBAND. (*suddenly embarrassed*) No. Nothing. Sorry. Come on. . . .

I. Hang on . . .

MYSELF. Wait . . .

ME. No. Tell me.

(*HUSBAND sits. A pause. ME waits patiently.*)

I. (*whispering*) What's happening?

MYSELF. (*whispering*) I think he's gone to sleep again . . .

HUSBAND. Funny you—remembering that orange juice . . .

ME. (*smiling*) Yes . . .

HUSBAND. And those dances . . .

ME. Yes.

HUSBAND. God. Weren't they awful . . . ?

I. Thanks.

HUSBAND. I didn't mean us. We weren't awful. They were. The dances. Awful. You know what I mean . . .

ME. Yes.

MYSELF. What the hell's he talking about?

HUSBAND. That's how we met wasn't it? At one of those do's?

ME. That's where I first saw you. You never saw me.

HUSBAND. Yes, I did. I asked you to dance.

ME. You didn't.

HUSBAND. I did.

ME. You never even noticed me . . .

HUSBAND. Of course I did. You were the only decent looking woman in the place . . .

ME. You danced with Caroline Liversedge . . .

MYSELF. Now, very fat, married, 5 kids . . .

ME. . . . Jeanette Finch . . .

I. Divorced twice. Varicose veins. Drinks . . .

ME. . . . and Pamela Hitchforth . . .

MYSELF. Lost at sea on a cross-channel ferry whilst on a secret weekend with her best friend's husband . . .

HUSBAND. You mean to say you remember all these women?

ME. Oh, yes . . .

HUSBAND. I'm blowed if I do. Pamela Hitchforth?

ME. Oh, I used to watch you. You've no idea . . .

I. Don't tell him everything. He'll get more conceited than ever . . .

HUSBAND. We didn't meet at the dances, then?

ME. No. We never danced. Not till much later.

MYSELF. If he'd found out how you danced he'd never have married you . . .

HUSBAND. When then?

ME. What?

HUSBAND. When did we meet?

ME. You mean when did *you* first notice *me* . . . ?

HUSBAND. OK. If you like. When?

I. In the butcher's . . .

MYSELF. So it was. The butcher's. Very romantic.

ME. Oh. In some shop.

HUSBAND. What shop?

ME. Oh, I don't remember now . . .

MYSELF. Liar . . .

HUSBAND. Hang on. I do. It was the butcher's, wasn't it?

ME. Oh, was it?

HUSBAND. On the corner of Rope Street . . .

I. He would remember that bit, wouldn't he? Can't remember me but he doesn't forget his pork chops.

ME. Yes. Possibly it was.

HUSBAND. We both happened to be in there. I was buying — that's right — pork chops . . . And you didn't have enough money with you. And I lent you some . . .

ME. Eighteen p.

HUSBAND. Ah, you do remember . . .

ME. Vaguely.

I. She remembers the dates of the coins.

HUSBAND. That's where we met. Just by chance . . .

ME. Yes . . .

HUSBAND. (*suspiciously*) Or was it some crafty ruse of yours? For us to meet? Accidentally on purpose?

ME. God, no . . .

HUSBAND. No?

[MUSIC #II–6: *HAVE YOU EVER THOUGHT?*]

ME. No . . .
HAVE YOU EVER THOUGHT
IT'S AT MOMENTS LIKE THESE
THAT YOU WANT TO SIT DOWN AND CRY?
JUST WHEN I WAS SURE
THERE WAS NO ONE I'D MEET
I LOOK UP AND CATCH YOUR EYE.
THIS WAS MY STAYING-HOME DAY,
ALL THOSE SMALL DOMESTIC CHORES.
SOMETIMES LIFE CAN BE SO CRUEL.
WASN'T IT JUST
BOUND TO HAPPEN
YOU'D SEE ME
WITH DIRTY HAIR, WITHOUT MY LENSES?
IF I'VE DUE WARNING
BELIEVE ME, I LOOK STUNNING.

HAVE YOU EVER THOUGHT
OF THE HOURS THAT I'VE SPENT
JUST IN CASE YOU SAW ME FIRST?
NEVER DID I DREAM
WE'D BE MEETING LIKE THIS
WHEN I KNEW I'D LOOK MY WORST.
I CAN LOOK QUITE ATTRACTIVE,
CAN'T YOU WAIT AN HOUR OR TWO?
JUST MY LUCK THAT THIS WOULD HAPPEN.
ISN'T IT JUST
SO DEPRESSING?
THE ONE DAY
I WASN'T WEARING ANY MAKE UP.
WON'T YOU HAVE MERCY?
PRETEND YOU HAVEN'T SEEN ME?
   HUSBAND.
HAVE YOU NEVER THOUGHT
THAT AT MOMENTS LIKE THESE
WHAT I WANT TO SEE, I SEE?
YOU MUST TRY AND SEE
THAT THE WOMAN I SEE

IS THE ONE I LOVE TO SEE . . .

(*HUSBAND and ME as before. All are silent for a moment.*)

HUSBAND. So.
ME. Oh.
MYSELF. Ah.
I. Mmm.
HUSBAND. Anyway . . .
ME. Yes . . .
MYSELF. Yes . . .
I. Yes . . .
HUSBAND. I was thinking. With regard to us . . . And so on . . .
ME. Yes?
HUSBAND. I think we must . . . I think I must try and make the effort a bit more. I don't think I've been making the effort lately . . .
ME. No. Nor me.
I. I have . . .
HUSBAND. So. What do you say? Make the effort, shall we?
ME. —Er . . .
I. Put it to the vote . . .
MYSELF. To the vote . . .
I. All those in favour . . .

(*ME, MYSELF and I all raise their hands.*)

MYSELF. Carried . . .
HUSBAND. (*staring at ME*) What are you doing?
ME. Arm's gone to sleep.
HUSBAND. You do need a check up.
ME. No, I don't, OK, then.
HUSBAND. OK what?
ME. Let's all make the effort. Fine.
HUSBAND. Good. Good. (*awkwardly*) Look, I promise I'll —
ME. (*smiling*) Yes, I promise, too . . .
I. I don't.
MYSELF. Sssh!
HUSBAND. While we can . . .
ME. While we can . . .

[MUSIC #II – 7: *ANOTHER BITE*]

HUSBAND.
YOU'LL FIND YOU'RE RARELY GIVEN SECOND
CHANCES.
YOU PAYS YOUR PIPER AND YOU DANCE YOUR
DANCES.
ONE MISTAKE,
YOUR LIFE IS SPENT REGRETTING IT—
NO HOPE OF YOU FORGETTING IT—
YOU SOW IT AND LOOK WHAT YOU REAP.
AND DEPENDING HOW YOU MADE YOUR BED IS
HOW YOU'LL SLEEP.
THERE'S A GREAT UNWRITTEN LAW THAT WILL
ENSURE YOU'LL NEVER

GET ANOTHER BITE
OF THE APPLE.
GET ANOTHER START
TO RELIVE IT ALL AGAIN.
HAVE ANOTHER RIDE
FOR YOUR PENNY—
THERE'LL BE NO SECOND CHANCE . . .

ME.
SO MY ADVICE IS GET IT RIGHT THE FIRST TIME.
A LITTLE CAUTION'S SURELY NOT THE WORST
CRIME—
CAREFULLY—
DON'T MARRY IN A FRYING PAN,
REMEMBER ALL YOUR CRYING CAN-
NOT PUT OUT THE FIRE THAT'S BENEATH
AND THE ONLY WAY YOU'LL SAVE YOUR SKIN
IS BY YOUR TEETH.
THERE'S A BASIC FACT OF LIFE
THAT GUARANTEES YOU'LL NEVER
GET ANOTHER BITE
OF THE APPLE—
GET ANOTHER START
TO RELIVE IT ALL AGAIN.
HAVE ANOTHER RIDE
FOR YOUR PENNY.

THERE'LL BE NO SECOND CHANCE—
   Me/Husband.
OF ANOTHER BITE
OF THE APPLE—
OF ANOTHER START
TO RELIVE IT ALL AGAIN.
OF ANOTHER RIDE
FOR YOUR PENNY.
THERE'LL BE NO SECOND CHANCE—
   Myself/I.
AND SINCE THE MOVIE ONLY HAS ONE SCREENING,
WE'D BEST INVEST IT WITH A DEEPER MEANING.
TREASURE IT,
EXPLOIT IT AND ENVELOP IT
ENLARGE IT AND DEVELOP IT,
WE'RE LUCKY WE'VE ALL GOT THIS FAR . . .
SO FORGET THE WAY THINGS COULD HAVE BEEN,
IT'S WHAT WE ARE.
THERE'S A UNIVERSAL TRUTH THAT PLAINLY
   STATES
WE'LL NEVER
GET ANOTHER BITE
OF THE APPLE—
GET ANOTHER START
TO RELIVE IT ALL AGAIN.
HAVE ANOTHER RIDE
FOR OUR PENNY,
THERE'LL BE NO SECOND CHANCE—

   All.
OF ANOTHER BITE
OF THE APPLE—
OF ANOTHER START
TO RELIVE IT ALL AGAIN.
OF ANOTHER RIDE
FOR OUR PENNY
WE'LL GET NO SECOND CHANCE—
YOU AND ME . . .

(*HUSBAND and ME as before.*)

   Husband. Have you got ten p?

ME. (*fumbling in her bag*) Yes, why?

HUSBAND. I'm just going to phone Mrs. Brown. Ask her if she'd mind looking after the kids till tea time.

ME. Why?

HUSBAND. Well, I thought we might go out . . .

ME. Out?

MYSELF. He's flipped.

I. He's gone.

HUSBAND. Yes. Just for a bit.

ME. What about your meeting?

HUSBAND. Oh, well . . . They'll get on without me. If they don't buy the bloody things, they don't buy them . . .

MYSELF. Emergency! Beep . . . beep . . . beep . . .

I. Husband out of control . . .

MYSELF. Emergency!

ME. Where are we going to?

HUSBAND. I don't know. Where you like. Just out somewhere. The two of us . . .

I. Four of us . . .

HUSBAND. What do you say?

MYSELF. (*together*) Yahoo!

I.   Whoopeee!

ME. Tell me something.

HUSBAND. Yes?

ME. Would you prefer me if I was someone else or do you like me to be myself . . . ?

I. This could be trouble?

HUSBAND. (*after a moment's reflection*) I like you when you're you . . .

MYSELF. There's no answer to that . . .

ME. Come on then . . . (*she starts to leave*)

HUSBAND. Hey. (*ME stops.*) Here a tick . . .

ME. (*coming to him*) What? (*HUSBAND makes to kiss her.*) Bill! Not here . . . People are . . .

MYSELF. Ssssh!

I. Don't stop him, you fool . . .

HUSBAND. Come here. Mum of the Year . . .

(*They kiss. MYSELF and I ecstatically share the kiss with ME.*)

MYSELF. (*together*) Mmmmmm!

I.   Aaaaah!

[MUSIC #II-8: *ME, MYSELF AND I (REPRISE)*]

REPORTER.
IS IT REALLY TRUE YOU BACKED EVERY WINNER—?
DID YOU FLY TO ROME ESPECIALLY FOR DINNER—?
HOW IS IT YOU EAT AND SEEM TO GET THINNER—?
DID YOU TELL THE DUKE HE'S JUST A BEGINNER—?
I.
YOU ASK THE QUESTIONS
I WILL REPLY
ALWAYS PROVIDING,
YOU LET ME TALK
ABOUT
ME, MYSELF AND I.
TAKE A LOOK
YOU CAN'T TELL IF THEY'RE REAL
AS I SLOWLY REVEAL
ALL MY HIDDEN
ASSETS.
REPORTER.
DID YOU POUR YOUR SOUP ON SOMEONE YOU
    HATED—?
DID YOU SAY THAT TOLSTOY'S MUCH
    OVERRATED—?
WERE YOU NOT THE BRIDE WHO ONCE
    DOUBLE-DATED—?
WERE YOU THAT UPSET YOUR MOVIE WAS
    SLATED—?

ME.	I.
ME, I'LL BE HONEST	CAN YOU TELL US WHY YOUR MARRIAGE HAS ENDED?
BRUTALLY FRANK	WHAT ABOUT THIS GREEK YOU'VE LATELY BEFRIENDED?
ME, I CAN TELL IT	IS IT REALLY TRUE YOUR HEART NEVER MENDED?
JUST AS IT WAS,	HOW ABOUT THE PRIEST THEY SAY YOU'VE OFFENDED?

THE TRUTH
I.
. .UNVARNISHED. .
ME.
ME, MYSELF AND I
I.
. .EXCLUSIVE. .
ME.
WHAT A JOY—
I.
. .IT'S BLISSFUL. .
ME.
—NOW I'M FREE TO
  REGALE
EVERY LURID
DETAIL
WHAT A CHANCE TO

AIR MY

FEELINGS
THE FIRST TIME
  ANYONE'S ASKED FOR
  MY
OPINION
FOR THOUGHTS ON
  EVERYTHING
ONLY TEN P.
READ IT IN ME, MYSELF
  ME/I.
AND I.
MYSELF.
NOW IS MY CHANCE TO

SPEAK FOR MYSELF

ALL MY AMBITIONS

ALL OF MY PLANS

I.
READ ALL ABOUT IT
YOU WON'T GET A
  CHANCE LIKE THIS
AGAIN TO CREEP INSIDE
  MY INMOST
FEELINGS
AND FANCIES

READ ALL
ABOUT IT

ME.
WILL YOU DARE DENY
  THE RUMOURS
  THEY'RE SPREADING?
IS IT REALLY TRUE YOU
  STREAKED AT YOUR
  WEDDING?
DO YOU STILL REGARD
  YOUR HUSBANDS AS
  BEDDING?
HOW IS YOUR CAREER

AND WHERE IS IT
HEADING?

(Simultaneously with ME, above:)

I.
CAN YOU TELL US WHY
  YOUR MARRIAGE HAS
  ENDED?
WHAT ABOUT THIS
  GREEK YOU'VE
  LATELY BEFRIENDED?
IS IT REALLY TRUE
  YOUR HEART NEVER
  MENDED?
HOW ABOUT THE PRIEST
  THEY SAY YOU'VE
  OFFENDED?

HUSBAND.
WILL YOU GIVE ME
  YOUR PERMISSION TO
  QUOTE YOU?
ARE WE FREE TO PRINT
  THE LETTER HE
  WROTE YOU?
DID YOU EVER FEEL THE
  BOARD WOULD OUT-
  VOTE YOU?
SAY YOU'D TELL HIS
  WIFE UNLESS HE'D
  PROMOTE YOU?

MYSELF.
THE FACTS
ME/I.
. .UNTARNISHED. .
MYSELF.
ME, MYSELF AND I
ME/I.
. .EXPOSE. .
MYSELF.
NOW AT LAST
ME/I.
. .AT LONG LAST. .
MYSELF.
ALL MY HOPES AND
  FEARS
HOW I BROKE DOWN IN

TEARS,

ME.
READ IT IN YOUR PAPER.
I.
READ ALL ABOUT IT.

MYSELF.
HOW MY LIFE'S
  BEEN

I.
YOU WON'T
  GET A
  CHANCE LIKE
  THIS

ME.
MAKING A
  CLEAN
  BREAST OF. .

FILLED WITH   AGAIN TO   GET THEM OFF
                 CREEP INSIDE   MY CHEST.
              MY INMOST
  MYSELF.   I/ME.
LAUGHTER   FEELINGS
I'LL UNBURDEN MYSELF   AND FANCIES
  OF ALL MY
  SECRETS   READ ALL
SO GET YOUR COPY NOW   ABOUT IT
TURN TO PAGE THREE
READ ABOUT—
  ME.
ME
  MYSELF.
MYSELF
  I.

AND I.   ME.
                FOR FURTHER DETAILS
                PLEASE SEE YOUR
                LOCAL
                ME/MYSELF/I.
                PAPER.
                IT'S THE ONE THE
                  WORLD'S WAITING TO
                  SEE
                WRITTEN BY
                  ME.
                ME
                  ME/MYSELF.
                MYSELF
                  ME/MYSELF/I.
                AND I.

CURTAIN

Other Publications for Your Interest

ANGRY HOUSEWIVES
(LITTLE THEATRE—MUSICAL)
Book & Lyrics by A.M. COLLINS
Music & Lyrics by CHAD HENRY

4 men, 4 women—Various sets.

Bored with their everyday, workaday lives and kept in insignificance by their boyfriends/husbands—these really are four *angry* housewives. They try a number of things in search of personal fulfillment, but nothing strikes a chord until one of them strikes a chord on her guitar, and gets the idea that, well, why don't they form a punk-rock group and enter the upcoming talent show down at the neighborhood punk club? Of course they form the group, of course they enter, and of course they win, calling themselves—of course—"The Angry Housewives", winning the contest—and stopping the show—with their punk-rock song. This genial satire of contemporary feminism ran for ages in Seattle, and has had numerous successful productions cross-country. "The show is insistently outrageous, frequently funny, occasionally witty and altogether irresistible."—Seattle Times. Slightly Restricted. **Posters.**

(#3931)

NUNSENSE
(LITTLE THEATRE—MUSICAL)
By DAN GOGGIN

5 women—Unit sets.

This delightful Off Broadway hit will certainly tickle your audience's funnybone. It's about the efforts of the Order of the Little Sisters of Hoboken (a nunnery, of course) to raise money to bury the remaining four of the fifty-two nuns who have died of botulism contracted by eating vichysoise prepared by the convent chef, Sister Julia (Child of God). Our five nuns have somehow been spared the fate of the other sisters, as they were playing bingo that night at another parish. *Nunsense*, then, is the fund-raising show they are presenting to us in hopes we will help them with the necessary cash. ". . . a lively 'nunstop' musical."—N.Y. Times. One of the feistiest shows around."—WNEW-TV. "Clever and amusing."—Catholic Transcript. "Good-natured. A cheerful evening."—Catholic Standard. Winner, 1986 Outer Critics Circle Award. Best Off-Broadway Musical. Slightly Restricted.

(#16074)

Other Publications for Your Interest

A . . . MY NAME IS ALICE
(LITTLE THEATRE—REVUE)
Conceived by JOAN MICKLIN SILVER and JULIANNE BOYD

5 women—Bare stage with set pieces

This terrific new show definitely rates an "A"—in fact, an "A-*plus*"! Originally produced by the Women's Project at the American Place Theatre in New York City, "Alice" settled down for a long run at the Village Gate, off Broadway. When you hear the songs, and read the sketches, you'll know why. The music runs the gamut from blues to torch to rock to wistful easy listening. There are hilarious songs, such as "Honeypot" (about a Black blues singer who can only sing about sex euphemistically) and heartbreakingly beautiful numbers such as "I Sure Like the Boys". A . . . *My Name is Alice* is a feminist revue in the best sense. It could charm even the most die-hard male chauvinist. "Delightful . . . the music and lyrics are so sophisticated that they can carry the weight of one-act plays".—NY Times. "Bright, party-time, pick-me-up stuff . . . Bouncy music, witty patter, and a bundle of laughs".—NY Post.   (#3647)

I'M GETTING MY ACT TOGETHER AND TAKING IT ON THE ROAD
(ALL GROUPS—MUSICAL)
Book and Lyrics by GRETCHEN CRYER
Music by NANCY FORD

6 men, 4 women—Bare stage

This new musical by the authors of *The Last Sweet Days of Isaac* was a hit at Joseph Papp's Public Theatre and transferred to the Circle-in-the-Square theatre in New York for a successful off-Broadway run. It is about a 40-year-old song writer who wants to make a come-back. The central conflict is between the song writer and her manager. She wants to include feminist material in her act—he wants her to go back to the syrupy-sweet, non-controversial formula which was once successful. "Clearly the most imaginative and melodic score heard in New York all season."—Soho Weekly News. "Brash, funny, very agreeable in its brash and funny way, and moreover, it touches a special emotional chord for our times."—N.Y. Post.   (#11025)